for Precious Little Girls and
their Furry Friends

Project
Precious Paws

By Cindy Kenney
Illustrated by the Precious Moments Creative Studio

Precious Moments # 990019 (Hardcover)
                # 990020 (Softcover)

Library of Congress Control Number: 2009920415

ISBN 978-0-9817159-4-0 (Softcover)
ISBN 978-0-9817159-5-7 (Hardcover)

Printed in China

Table of Contents

Chapter One: Girl's Best Friend 1

Chapter Two: Lost and Found 7

Chapter Three: It's Not Easy Being Purr-fect..............14

Chapter Four: Project Precious Paws..................20

Chapter Five: A Class Act 29

Chapter Six: Friends Fur-Ever. 37

Chapter Seven: Chasing Your Tail
    Gets You Nowhere......................... 44

Chapter Eight: Let Sleeping Dogs Lie 49

Chapter Nine: Raining Cats and Dogs.............. 60

Chapter Ten: Busy as a Bee 67

Chapter Eleven: Can You Teach an Old Dog
    New Tricks?....................................72

Chapter Twelve: In the Dog House 76

Chapter Thirteen: Look What the Cat
    Dragged In....................................80

Chapter Fourteen: A Dog Gone Success 83

CHAPTER ONE

Girl's Best Friend

"Weeeeeeeee!" I giggled, sliding across the glistening ice on Lake Lightning. It was a cold but beautiful day in Shine, Wisconsin, where we had moved last summer. I was heading to a Saturday meeting of the Precious Girls Club, a group my mom and aunt helped me start so I could meet new friends and use my talents to help others. Being in the club is the most fun I have ever had in my life!

"Whoaaaa!" I shouted as my feet slipped out from underneath me, and I landed on my bottom. "Yowch! That smarts."

The ice was super cold against my jeans, so I rolled over to stand up but saw the ice start to crack beneath me. I suddenly remembered Aunt Ella's warning about not walking on the ice unless the green flags were posted for ice-skating. I quickly glanced at the shoreline; the flags were red!

The crack got deeper, even without my moving. Water started seeping through, and within seconds my mittens and knees were soaked. *Oh no!* I thought. *What am I going to do?* As I searched the shore for someone to help, the ice broke and my legs plunged into the icy water.

"Help!" I screamed, clawing at the shiny surface. No one was around!

"Hang in there, kiddo," came the sound of a comforting whisper in my ear. It was my guardian angel.

"Faith! What should I do? Help me!" I shrieked. "I'm so scared. I've never been this scared before—ever!"

"You will be okay, Katie. You must have faith, sweetie," she said, trying to keep me calm.

That was hard. I tried to kick my freezing legs and pull myself up onto the ice, but the water was so cold it made them feel achy and heavy.

"Hang in there, Munchkin," Faith said again.

I am the only one who can see and hear Faith, so I knew she could not go and get someone.

Then I heard a noise behind me. Faith was right. I was so excited as I turned around to reach for whomever had come up to help.

"Ahhhhhhh! Nooo!" I screamed, slipping a little farther into the water. Hot tears streamed down my cold cheeks. A big dirty dog had wandered out onto the ice, and I was afraid he was going to bite me or push me all the way in.

"Please! Somebody help!" I screamed again.

"Woof! Woof!" The dog's loud bark scared me and made me lose my grip on the ice.

"Ahhhh!" I yelled, losing my grip a bit more. My shout seemed to frighten the dog, because he jumped back and quickly pranced back to the shore. I continued to yell for help, but no one was around. "Faith, I don't know how long I can hold on. The water is so c-c-cold!" My teeth were chattering and my legs felt numb.

"Oh, no!" I cried. "He's coming back!" *Dear God, please, please help me to stay safe. I don't know what to do and I need Your help,* I prayed.

The yucky, brown-and-white dog headed back toward me. I tried to slide away from him, but he followed me around the icy circle. He was coming after me!

"Woof! Woof! Ahrr . . . ahrr . . . ahrr," the dog whined. It was not a scary sound, and when I looked up, he dropped a big stick right in front of me.

"I don't want to play fetch," I cried. "Go get help!" My tears were freezing along the creases in my neck, I could not stop them from pouring down my face.

The dog nudged the stick closer with his nose, continuing to whine gently. When it was right beside my hand, I reached out to grab it, as he snatched the other end in his jaws and pulled. Part of my frozen body lifted up out of the water, and I got a better grip on the ice. But my legs were so numb that I could not move or lift myself back onto the surface.

The scruffy dog kept pulling on the stick to keep me from falling in for a long time, or at least it felt like it.

Then finally I heard someone shout, "Hey! Call for help! Someone has fallen through the ice!"

A whole rescue team surrounded me pretty fast after that. No one was around when I fell through the ice, but suddenly the entire shore filled with people waiting to see what would happen.

A man carefully edged out onto the ice on his belly

and tossed me a big rope. He told me to put it over my head and put my arm through the loop. I was afraid to let go of the stick, because the dog was keeping me from falling deeper into the water.

The rescue man saw my worried face, so he spoke to me in a really calm voice. He thought the dog was mine, because he said, "Your doggie is doing a good job of taking care of you. He won't let go. Use your other arm to put the rope around you."

I looked at him and then at the dog. My heart was thumping hard inside my chest, and I was scared to let go. The rescue man kept telling me to take the rope, so I finally let go of the ice and grabbed it. My other hand kept hold of the stick, and the dog kept me from falling into the water the whole time.

Within seconds they lifted me up out of the water, and I had paramedics putting lots of blankets on me. Then I got to ride in the ambulance!

CHAPTER TWO

Lost and Found

"Surprise, Katie!" everyone shouted as I walked through the door. Everybody was standing in my living room—all my friends from the Precious Girls Club, my family, Patches, Miss Marla, my teacher and of course Faith was there too.

"Oh, my goodness!" I was so surprised and happy to see all my friends. My knees were sort of shaking, and Daddy grabbed hold of my shoulders to keep me from falling.

"Hi, Katie! We all missed you very much," Miss Marla said. She handed me a great big card that my class had made. Everybody had signed it.

I was in the hospital for several days, but everything turned out okay, thanks to a very special dog that saved my life. Faith said she was proud of me, because I had had faith and had never given up.

"Come on, let's have some fun!" Mom said.

I love parties. Who doesn't? This one was really fun! We played games and made pretty beaded hair ribbons, and Aunt Ella made one of her famous deluxe brownie supreme recipes. Everybody wanted the recipe.

Then came an even bigger surprise! As soon

as the party was over, a reporter and photographer from the *Shine Times* stopped by to interview me. She wanted the whole story about how the dog rescued me from Lake Lightning. Then we went over to the Precious Paws Animal Shelter where they were taking care of the dog.

"Here he is," said Mr. Duncan, director of the shelter. "No one claimed him. When they brought him in, he was in bad shape—thirsty, hungry. One of his legs has some cuts on it, but they should heal up fairly nice. Your Aunt Ella has been over to help me care for him all week."

The brown-and-white dog no longer looked like the scary beast that first scared me, but then came to my rescue on the ice. Now he was nice and clean.

"Look, Mom, he remembers me!"

The dog wagged his tail and looked happier than the last time I had seen him. "Woof! Woof!"

"Come here, Moses," I said.

The man let go of his collar and Moses pranced over to see me. He was so gentle and started to lick my hands and nuzzle up against me.

"How do you know his name is Moses?" the reporter asked.

"Oh, ummm . . . I really don't. I thought of that name when I was in the hospital. God helped Moses rescue His people from slavery in Egypt, and this guy rescued me when I was trapped in the ice. It's one of my favorite Bible stories. So I was thinking it would be a cool name for this fella too. Is that okay?" I looked at Mr. Duncan and he nodded his head. "Great! What do you think, boy? I think he likes it too."

"You're right," Aunt Ella agreed. "It's a wonderful name, Katie. Well done."

The photographer took our picture, and then Aunt Ella joined us. She agreed to adopt Moses and take him home. I was so glad he was going to have a nice home. Plus I'd get to see him all the time.

Mr. Duncan excused himself to answer a phone call, and when he returned, he looked upset. "Please excuse me, but I just got an emergency call about an abandoned cat and a litter of kittens."

"Oh no! Why don't people take care of their animals?" I asked. "Why are people so depictable?"

"*Despicable* you mean?" Mr. Duncan laughed. "Lots of reasons, kiddo. I'm afraid I don't have time to explain right now, but I'll tell you some other time. Is that okay?"

I nodded. "Hey, what if the newspaper did a story on *that?*" I asked.

The reporter thought for a minute and agreed to go with Mr. Duncan to get the kittens.

"That's great!" Mr. Duncan said. "But now I have to run out to get them. There's never enough help around here to do everything."

"We understand. We'll come back later to complete the paperwork on Moses," my dad told him.

"Thanks, so much."

"Can we do anything to help?" my mom asked.

"Be careful, I may take you up on it," Mr. Duncan smiled.

We agreed to stay and help while Mr. Duncan

was gone. He told us there were checklists of duties on clipboards in the animal rooms and to do whatever we could until he got back.

After he left we walked back to where they kept the animals. I couldn't believe it! There were dogs and cats of every shape, size, and color—room after room, filled with unwanted animals that needed someone to love them. The shelter also had bunnies, birds, turtles, frogs, gerbils, and even two chickens.

"Faith, look at all of these animals. Why doesn't anybody want them?" I asked.

Faith flitted from cage to cage, pausing to cuddle with a kitten, pet a dog, whisper something to a bird, or just give an animal a hug. "The better question is: what are *you* going to do to help?" she asked.

"Who, me?" I giggled.

"Yes, you!"

"What can I do? I'm just a kid."

"Then who?" she asked. "Think about it."

CHAPTER THREE

It's Not Easy Being Purr-fect

"I'll get it!" I called from the kitchen and stood to reach for the phone.

"Was that Mr. Duncan?"

"Yes. He thanked us for all the work we did at the Precious Paws Shelter."

"How are the kittens?" Anna asked.

"He doesn't know yet. Somebody left them in a box in the alley near the paper mill. They were there a long time and were in really bad shape."

"Poor little things! Daddy, can we have one?" Anna asked. "Please?"

"Honey, we can't adopt all of the animals. You wanted us to bring home another dog and two bunnies when we left," Daddy said.

"I know you mean well, Anna," Mom added, "but caring for an animal is a lot of responsibility."

"I would take care of it, honest!"

"It takes more than that, honey. We don't know if a cat would get along with Patches. And believe it or not, you'll be leaving to go to college . . ." Mom sighed. "It's hard to even think about that day!"

We all looked at each other and laughed.

"Now that we're talking about responsibility," Daddy interrupted, "we need to discuss your fall through the ice. Katie, you're old enough to be more responsible about listening to directions and reading signs. Your school and Aunt Ella taught you about being responsible around the ice on the lake."

"I know, Daddy. I'm sorry. I won't let it happen again."

"Good," he said. "You learned a difficult lesson. In fact, walking on thin ice is a lot like going through the day without being responsible. When you act irresponsibly, you never know when the ice will break and everything will fall apart."

"Yes sir, you're right."

"You know, there is something I would like you to do for me."

"What is it, Daddy?"

"Make lists of all the things you've done that you think are responsible and irresponsible. It's important that you evaluate your everyday decisions so that you have a clear understanding of how important it is to be responsible in everything you do."

"I can do that, Daddy."

"Good. I think that's a good start toward planning for the future too," he said.

"You are so lucky that Moses was there to help you until someone came," Mom said, giving me a little hug from behind. "God was watching over you that day."

Faith did a little twirl in the center of the table, then winked and blew me a kiss. I remembered how she told me to have faith that day.

"I will be more responsible. I promise."

"The next Precious Girls Club is at our house this week, and the group is looking for another project. Do you think the girls would like to do something for the Precious Paws Animal Shelter?"

"That's a super idea, Mom. I think the girls would love that."

"Wonderful! I'll tell your Aunt Ella."

"How fun! I can't wait to tell the other girls."

"In the meantime, head upstairs and give some thought to those lists, okay?" Daddy asked.

"Okay, I will."

Upstairs, it was nice to have a talk with Faith. Although she was with me at the hospital, we did not get to talk much. Someone was always going in or out of my room. Late at night she would sing to me, though. Faith has the loveliest voice I've ever heard.

After we talked she zoomed toward my desk and landed right on a spiral notebook. "All right, Munchkin, let's get to work on those lists for your dad. And don't roll your eyes at me. You got off easy. Come on, let's see what you come up with."

Faith always encouraged me to get things done. I don't know what I'd do without her. I went over to my desk and sat down. Hmmmm, I thought for a bit and then started to write. Once I did I was surprised how many things I did everyday that involved being responsible.

Responsibility

- ❏ I do my chores
- ❏ I take Patches for walks and feed him
- ❏ I do my homework
- ❏ I help my Aunt Ella in the store
- ❏ I obey the rules most of the time
- ❏ I go to school and church
- ❏ I use my talents to do good things
- ❏ I help to entertain kids at the hospital
- ❏ I say my prayers every night

Irresponsibility

- ❑ I lost ten dollars
- ❑ I overslept and was late for school once
- ❑ I ate too much candy last Halloween
- ❑ I let my girlfriend cut my hair when I was five
- ❑ I didn't brush my teeth all the time and got a cavity
- ❑ I put marshmallows on my pizza and wasted food
- ❑ I broke the swing by climbing where I shouldn't have
- ❑ I spilled grape juice on the carpet
- ❑ I didn't rake Mrs. Fisher's lawn when I promised I would
- ❑ I didn't study for a math test
- ❑ I didn't stay off the ice

CHAPTER FOUR

Project Precious Paws

Everyone spoke all at once when my mom and Aunt Ella presented the idea about helping the Precious Paws Animal Shelter as our next project. The girls were excited!

"Keep in mind that making this commitment will be a big responsibility, girls," Aunt Ella reminded us. "Mr. Duncan said there are several ways that you can help. Whatever you choose, he would like it to be something you will enjoy and carry through with."

Everyone tossed out a bunch of ideas.

"What if we do a fundraiser for the shelter?" I asked. "It would be an awesome way to let everybody know how many animals need our help. Plus it's a great way to get the community involved in taking responsibility for doing something about it."

"That's a good point, Katie," Aunt Ella agreed.

Faith waved to me from where she was sitting on the piano. She thought it was a good idea too. After we talked, we voted to do it.

"Look everybody! Ruffles likes the idea too. She hasn't stopped purring since we began," Kirina

giggled. When she and her family had heard about the abandoned kittens, they had gone over to adopt one. She had white wavy fur mixed into darker gray fur that looked like ruffles all down her back. It was a perfect name, and all the girls adored her.

"I want a turn holding the kitten," Jenny said.

Jenny had come a long way toward being nicer to the other girls in the group, but lately she was starting to act bossy again. Ruffles seemed to soften her a bit though. She got quieter as the cute furry kitten started to nuzzle up against her and purr.

"If you girls undertake a big project like a fundraiser, I would recommend that you choose someone to be in charge of it," Aunt Ella suggested.

Everyone agreed, but no one volunteered.

"Keep in mind that being the leader does not mean doing all of the work," Mom pointed out. "It just means organizing and providing a little guidance."

"I recommend Nicola," I said. "She's the oldest girl in the group, and she's super organized. She was president of her class, and she was the student director of the school play. Everybody said she did a terrific job at both!"

Becca and Avery agreed. Nicola blushed.

"Personally, I think *I* would be an excellent candidate for the position," Jenny spoke up. "After all, my daddy is president of the Shine Community Bank, and he owns the Shine Hardware Store. He can get many businesses to donate stuff for the auction. I should also point out that I am a straight-A student and have been on the honor roll ever since kindergarten. Put my name on the ballot too."

Everyone got quiet and felt a little uncomfortable. We all turned to my Mom and Aunt Ella, hoping they would know what to do.

"How lovely to have two such talented girls capable of doing such a big job," Aunt Ella gushed. "Fortunately, I don't think we need a ballot for something like this, and there will be many opportunities for everyone to take a turn at being leader as we do more projects. Let's allow Nicola to take the leadership role this time, because she is older, and perhaps Jenny can be in charge of the auction?"

It was a good solution, but I could tell that Jenny was fuming. She would not argue though, because she always came across as angelic in front of teachers and grown-ups.

"Excellent! It's settled," my Mom continued. "How about if I serve everyone some vegetables and fruit while you discuss what jobs to take?"

"Sounds great, Mom. Thanks!" I said.

As soon as the adults left the room, Jenny tossed Ruffles on Kirina's lap and said, "Fine, well I have to leave early. I have a lot to do."

"Don't get your britches in a bunch," Lidia said, causing most of the girls to giggle.

"I'm doing no such thing," Jenny said with a glare. "It just so happens that I have other important things to do. Not everything revolves around this little club you know."

"I wish it did!" Kirina said.

"Me too!"

"Me three!"

Jenny took off, but Nicola went after her.

"Yum! Mrs. Bennett, these look scrumptious," Avery said as the girls dug into the freshly cut fruit and veggies.

"Enjoy, girls. Where did Jenny and Nicola go? Are they already busy making plans?" Aunt Ella asked.

"Uhhhh, not exactly. Jenny got her britches in a bunch," I explained and burst out laughing with the others. I never heard such a funny saying before.

We told my mom and Aunt Ella what happened, and Mom said, "Now that's the sign of a good leader. Nicola took responsibility for helping out when someone felt hurt. You've got the right person for the job."

Nicola was not gone long.

"Why did you go after her?" Becca asked.

"She was upset. We need to work together

we all have to do our share. Besides, if she wants to be the leader, I don't mind."

"But we do!" I said and got a scowl from both my mom and Faith, who fluttered overhead.

"Well, you don't have to worry, because she isn't interested in being the leader anymore. I think she'll be in charge of the auction, though. You know her dad has provided a lot of help to our group in the past," Nicola pointed out.

Reluctantly, we all nodded.

"Let's think of different ways to make this fundraiser work. We all need to sign up for how we want to help, so we know who is doing what and how we can spread the word," Nicola said, changing the topic.

Not only was she a good leader, but she was also cheerful. She never stayed angry or down about any-thing. Of course, that's why I nominated her!

I can organize a bake sale," Bailey offered.

"Oooo, I can help with that too," Lidia said. "My grandma loves to bake, and she has yummy recipes."

"I can organize a craft fair," I volunteered. "I like making stuff. Aunt Ella, would you help me?"

"Nothing would make me happier, darlin'," she answered.

"I'll organize a talent show," Kirina offered. "Becca, would you help?"

She nodded.

"I can make sure that everyone is signed up to do things at the shelter so we'll be informed about what we're asking people to do," Avery said.

"Wow! You girls are taking on quite a bit," Aunt Ella warned. "That's a great deal of work. I think you could do any one of those things and the shelter would be delighted."

"We want to have an amazing fundraiser and really make a difference," Lidia said.

"I'm sure you will," my mom said. "Just be careful about extending yourselves too much. It's wonderful what you want to do, but if you try to do more than you can, that's irresponsible. If you fail, everyone will end up getting hurt in the long run."

We quietly considered what they said for a few minutes, but before long the chatter started again, and we moved forward with our plans. Project Precious Paws was underway!

CHAPTER FIVE

A Class Act

"Pass your study guides to the front of the class, please," Miss Marla said.

We all handed our papers forward and waited to see what we were going to do next.

"I have a surprise for you today," she announced. As you know the girls have been busy organizing a fundraiser for the Precious Paws Animal Shelter. Hopefully you've seen the posters and volunteered to help. It's going to be a community-wide event for Shine, Wisconsin."

Miss Marla pulled out a cage with the cutest little bunny. "This is Nibbles."

Everyone "Oooed" and "Ahhhed." But then she set the bunny down and picked up two more cages. The class got excited!

"Sit down, please," Miss Marla said, "so that everyone can see. Thank you. The turtle's name is

Speedy, and the hamster is Chip. Our class is going to be responsible for taking care of these animals. I will be adding each pet to our daily job chart so everyone will have a chance."

Miss Marla set Chip's cage down on Jenny's desk. Jenny turned to smirk at the rest of us.

Next she set Speedy down on Bailey's desk, but she didn't act so "la de da" about it.

"Ouch!" I said, quietly, feeling a little tug on my ear.

Faith whispered, "Be nice! Jenny is your friend, remember?" She flew a loop around my desk and zoomed out of the classroom.

She was right. I'd been trying to be nice to Jenny McBride, but it sure was hard sometimes. She always thought she was better than everybody else and tried so hard to boss us around.

"Hold on, everyone," Miss Marla said. "There's more!"

Everyone sat down and got quiet.

"I thought it would be fun to have a pet parade to help advertise the upcoming fundraiser for the Precious Paws Animal Shelter."

There were big cheers, hoots, and hollers!

"Settle down, please," Miss Marla reminded us. "I'm glad you like the idea, but not everyone owns a pet. Some of you have pets that would not be appropriate to bring to the community center for the parade. I arranged with Mr. Duncan at the Precious Paws Animal Shelter to let you adopt an animal for a day to be in the parade. You will need your parents' permission and must be responsible for that animal all day," she explained. "For those of you whose parents are not comfortable with that, you can bring in your favorite stuffed animal."

That part was lame. Nobody wanted to bring in a stuffed animal if everybody else would have a real one. Miss Marla handed out a sheet of instructions explaining when and where the parade would be and exactly what types of animals could participate.

Four other classes in our school were going to participate in the parade at the community center next Friday too. The kids talked about it all day at lunch, recess, and every other chance we had.

The Precious Girls Club met on the playground after school before we went home.

"This parade is going to be awesome!" Nicola

"Oh yum! I love baked stuff!" I said. "For the craft sale we put together a fun list of projects. Volunteers can come and make them at my Aunt Ella's store."

"What kinds of crafts, Katie?"

"You can make a bird house, a pet bed, a food or water bowl, or an animal photo frame and calendar. Plus you can make a crazy critter to play with or hang on your backpack. They're super cute!"

"I don't have a pet to bring for the parade, and I know my dad and stepmom aren't going to let me adopt one for a day," said Avery.

"Maybe they will if you tell them why we're doing this," Nicola encouraged.

"I doubt it. My mom has the new baby at home, so she's so worried somebody is going to come in contact with germs or something."

"At least you'll have lots of stuffed animals to pick from," Jenny said.

"Whoop-dee-do," Avery pouted.

"Well my dog is too big for the parade," Becca said. "But maybe my parents will let me adopt a smaller animal for the day."

"Jeremy Slavinski is going to adopt a snake. Can you believe it?" Kirina squealed.

"Ewwwwww!" most of the girls giggled.

"My grandpa used to work at a nature center," Lidia said. "He worked with snakes and frogs and stuff. He knows all kinds of things about nature."

"Who is trying out for the talent show from our group?" Nicola asked.

"I am, of course," Jenny said.

"Me too!" several others volunteered.

"I gotta get home," Bailey said. "Hey, Katie, I'll see you and Nicola at the shelter tonight. I think we're all on the schedule."

We wrapped things up and said good-bye. I wondered how I was going to get all my homework done on top of working at the shelter and helping Aunt Ella at the craft shop after school. *Oh well,* I thought. *I'm sure I'll figure something out.*

CHAPTER SIX

Friends Fur-ever!

"Did you hear how many things that parrot can say?" Bailey asked as I came out of the back room of the animal shelter.

"No, I haven't even seen the parrot yet. How did he wind up here?" I asked.

"He belonged to an older lady, who couldn't take care of him anymore."

"Wow, I never even thought about that before. I can't believe how many different reasons animals wind up here. Did you hear that most of the kittens were adopted?"

"That's awesome," she answered, finishing up washing the pet bowls. "I'm going to fill these water dishes, put them back, and then I have to go."

"But you're on the schedule until eight o'clock," I said.

"I have a ton of homework and got a C on a spelling test today. My mom will freak if my grades drop. She gets all upset when my grades go down."

"You mean she gets her britches in a bunch?" I laughed.

"Exactly."

"Well don't sign up for any other times that you can't stay. Mr. Duncan said that . . ."

"I know, Katie!" Bailey interrupted sharply. "I didn't know I was going to have this much homework."

She grabbed the dishes and stormed out of the room, nearly flattening Nicola as they collided in the doorway.

"What's she so upset about?" Nicola asked.

I told her what happened.

"Your mom and aunt may have been right about taking on too much," Nicola said when I was finished. "Some of the other girls are getting stressed out too. We may have taken on more than we should have."

I scowled at her.

"It's not that we don't want to help, Katie. It's just a lot of work. My parents didn't let me have a goldfish until I was in second grade because they didn't think I was ready. They finally caved in and bought me an aquarium with a few fish. They were dead within six months. I'd forget to feed them or didn't want to clean the tank. It was always something."

"Do you have any pets now?"

"I think my parents are going to let me get a puppy from the shelter!" she said excitedly. "They finally think I'll be responsible enough to take care of one."

"Really? That's super cool! Which one are you getting?"

"I can't decide. They are all so cute. I almost feel bad about picking one over the others."

As we laughed and talked about the different dogs, Mr. Duncan and his assistant burst through the door with the cutest little fluffy poodle and a very large, angry dog that looked as if he wanted to tear into us.

"Just stay calm," Mr. Duncan said when he saw the fear in our eyes. "No fast movements."

That was fine with me. I was not going to do anything to make that dog angrier.

"Did you see that little poodle?" Nicola gushed as the dogs disappeared into the back room.

"I guess so. I was concentrating more on the dog that wanted to eat me," I said, feeling as if I could breathe now.

"Don't worry, Mr. Duncan doesn't make us do anything we're uncomfortable doing. Plus he never has us signed up to work with a dog like that."

"You're right; besides, most of them are so nice. I have no idea how you're going to pick a dog," I laughed. "You really like working here, don't you?"

"I sure do. I've even thought about becoming a veterinarian. Or maybe I'll just work with Mr. Duncan right here at the shelter someday. Maybe I'll be his assistant director."

"You girls did a very nice job cleaning the bowls," Mr. Duncan said, returning from the animal area. "I appreciate your help."

"Why was that dog so ferocious?" I asked.

"Someone had tied him to a tree by an old farmhouse. No telling how long he had been there. And they hadn't been very nice to him."

"Oh, no!"

"Unfortunately, some people don't treat animals the way they should. It's very sad," he explained. "I try to work with them so that they aren't so frightened and angry with people anymore."

"What happens when you can't?" Nicola asked.

"Then they live right here at the shelter. We give them all the love and attention we can until we find them a home."

"People have been very surprised to hear how many animals you get every year," I said.

"It's pretty amazing," he agreed. "And we're just one shelter of thousands around the country. I can't thank the Precious Girls Club enough for all the help you're giving us."

"You're welcome," Nicola and I both answered at the same time.

"Do you realize how much the money you raise will help this shelter and the animals? I can purchase some new pet beds, some cages, and even food. Depending on how much is raised, I may even be able to hire a little more help so the animals will get more attention."

"That would be so nice," Nicola said. "We'll do our best, Mr. Duncan."

"I know. Speaking of which, would you girls like to walk a couple of dogs before you leave?"

"Sure!" we agreed.

Nicola walked a frisky beagle named Huckleberry, and I walked a yellow lab named Heidi. It was a lot of fun to walk and play with both dogs, and they were so happy to be outside.

As soon as we got back, we put the dogs away and left for home, but I got home later than usual. I suddenly remembered my homework and gulped. I had no idea how I was going to get it all done.

CHAPTER SEVEN

Chasing Your Tail Gets You Nowhere

The moonlight was streaming through my window as I studied for my math test, a subject I had so much trouble with no matter how hard I tried. Beneath my chair Patches was sleeping on my foot. I jumped when the door opened and Daddy came in to check on me.

"Hey, what's this?" he asked. "I thought you were in bed."

"I have a big math test tomorrow," I confessed.

"Then turn on your light so you can see better. It's a little hard to study with just a flashlight."

"Okay, Daddy. I just didn't want . . ."

"Us to find out?" he smiled. "Your mother told me that you've been gone ever since you got out of school today, first at Aunt Ella's craft shop, and then working at the shelter."

"Yes. I finished making the prettiest birdhouse today, Daddy. Wait till you see it! Aunt Ella showed me how to hammer it together yesterday, and I painted it today."

"Katie, I'm so proud of you and how hard you're working on your Precious Girls Club project. But I'm concerned that you're trying to do too much."

"I'm not!" I insisted. "Honest, Daddy. Besides, the fundraiser will be all over soon."

"Well, okay. I just want you to be careful how you handle your time. I don't want you to get sick or see your grades suffer."

"They won't."

"Okay, kiddo," he chuckled. "Well I miss having you around here in the evenings too. But you're having fun with this, aren't you?"

"Oh yes! I'm making all sorts of super-cool stuff at Aunt Ella's. And I really love taking care of the pets, Daddy. Nicola said she thinks she wants to be a veterinarian."

"Good for her. And I hear you're going to start the talent show with the help of Moses?"

"Yes, I guess."

"You'll do fine. I think it's wonderful. Now don't stay up too late, understood?"

"I won't."

Daddy kissed me and walked toward the door. "Don't forget to say your prayers."

"Okay. Goodnight."

A swirl of pastel colors and tiny white sparkles spun around my desk as Faith did a quick spin, a triple loop, and landed on my dictionary.

"You got off lucky, Munchkin," Faith said. "Are you sure you aren't in over your head?"

"Don't get your britches in a bunch, Faith," I giggled. "I'm getting everything done."

"Honest?"

"Okay, I'm a little busy. But it will all be over soon, Faith."

"But you signed up to work at the shelter even after it's over."

"I can handle it. Lots of kids have sports, dance, or music lessons."

"Just don't bite off more than you can chew. You don't want to get *your* britches in a bunch," she giggled.

"You should have seen the dogs they brought in tonight, Faith. One really scared me. Oh! And I got to walk the most beautiful yellow lab named Heidi. She was so fun to play with."

"That's a pretty name," Faith said.

"Oh, and you should have seen this poor Saint Bernard named Walter. He always looks so sad.

Mr. Duncan said he's been there for two years, but nobody has taken him home yet. And there's this sweet cat named Tuxedo. He purrs and purrs when you pet him, but nobody has adopted him either. I wish I could take a whole bunch of them home."

"You have a good heart, Katie," Faith said.

"It seems like no matter how much we do, it's never enough."

Faith sprang into motion and did a loop around my room and landed right back in front of me.

"That's why you have to have faith. Say a prayer for all those precious animals. God will watch over them too."

So that's what I did. I completed my math study and a worksheet for science. Then I climbed into bed and prayed for all the animals at the shelter. I asked God to bless our fundraiser and my friends in the Precious Girls Club. But as I nodded off to sleep, I realized I hadn't read a story that I was supposed to read by tomorrow. Uh oh. There was always something!

CHAPTER EIGHT

Let Sleeping Dogs Lie

Everyone was working hard on the fundraiser. Nicola was a terrific leader. She did a great job keeping everyone organized and on task. Even though we took on more than we should have as a club, it made many people aware of the animal shelter. Everywhere we went, people were buzzing about it.

"Katie Marie Bennett, I'm not going to call you again!" My mom called.

Morning came way too early. I was so tired and didn't want to get out of bed.

"Hey! Get up!" A different voice said as I felt a tug on my hair. I opened one eye to see Faith pulling on several tangled strands to get my attention. I waved her away.

"Come on, today is the pet parade!" Faith reminded me. She knew I was looking forward to it.

"Woof! Woof!" Patches barked in agreement. Anna was going to show him off at the parade, and I was planning on taking Moses.

"Okay," I yawned.

"I'm not going to wait for you again this morning," Anna said, poking her head inside my room. "You've been late every day this week."

I wanted to crawl back in bed and pull the covers over my head.

"Aren't you going to be late?" Mom asked when I finally made my way downstairs and put on my coat. "How is everything going for the fundraiser tomorrow night? Any problems?"

I looked at her and fibbed, "Everything is fine. I told you that yesterday."

"Okay, just checking," she said while looking at her watch. "You'd better hurry."

• • •

At school, everyone had ants in their pants. No one could sit still. Everybody was talking about the parade. They wanted to know who was going

50

to bring what animal. Pet names were exchanged, temporary and permanent pet adoption stories were traded, and even some of the crafts made at Aunt Ella's were shown off that day.

"Becca!" I whispered. "Hey, Becca!"

She had laid her head down on the desk and started to doze off. She quickly popped up and looked around to see who had spotted her.

"I didn't want you to get in trouble," I told her.

"Thanks. I didn't get much sleep last night. I had to finish my book report."

"Me too," I admitted. We all had a big report due today.

"I need your attention, please," Miss Marla said for the umpteenth time. "Some of you did not do too well on the grammar test and the pet essay. I marked your papers and if you need to make corrections, have them signed by a parent, and return them on Monday morning."

I knew what my test and paper would say before I got them back. A quick glance confirmed it. Both of them had to be signed, corrected, and returned. My mom and dad were not going to be pleased.

At lunch I found out I was not the only one of my friends who had to redo homework. We were all tired and running out of time with everything that had to be done for our big fundraiser tomorrow night.

"Why did you guys tell me everything was okay when it wasn't?" Nicola asked.

"I thought I had enough people to take care of everything," Kirina admitted. "I still don't have anyone to usher, do the programs, and the lighting guy just quit. Plus Mr. O'Tool said the band area has to be set up a certain way."

Nicola was carefully recording all of the problems we each reported the day before the big event. "Did you guys get cleanup crews for afterwards?" she asked Lidia and Bailey.

They both looked at one another in complete shock. Nicola shook her head and continued to write. "Avery, I got a call from Mr. Duncan last night saying that not all of the girls were meeting their commitments on the schedule you turned in."

"I didn't have time to call everyone this week. I just figured they'd remember to look at the schedule to figure it out," Avery complained.

"How are we supposed to look at the schedule when we're not there?" Kirina protested.

All of the girls erupted into a flurry of grumbling, pointing fingers, and whining.

"Stop it!" Nicola said. "Part of being responsible means owning up when we make a mistake and being honest about things. None of us have done a very good job at that lately."

Her words hit me sorta hard. She was right. I hadn't been very honest with my mom and dad this week when they asked how things were going. As the parent sponsors of this project, they had a right to know, and I was avoiding telling them the truth.

"Well *I'm* ready for tomorrow night," Jenny reported with a proud smile. "The auction will be perfect. The baskets look beautiful. Everything has been taken care of."

"That's because your daddy did all of it for you," Kirina said.

"Yeah, Jenny. How much work have you done?" Avery asked.

Once again the girls exploded with a combustion of chatter, complaints, and accusations. Nicola shook her head, closed her notebook, and walked away. I quickly got up and followed.

"What are we going to do?" I asked Nicola.

"I'm not sure," she said. "I don't know if we can pull this thing off."

"We have to! A ton of people are coming! And the pet parade is this afternoon."

"Katie, there are a ton of things that haven't been done, and we aren't prepared to take care of them. I'm not a miracle worker. I'm sorry, I need some time to think," she said.

I could tell she was doing her best to hold back tears. Nicola had worked very hard to try and pull this off, but no one had been straight with her. On top of it everyone was bickering.

As usual the bell rang indicating time was up and lunch was over.

• • •

The disappointment and gloominess of the morning gave way to laughter and fun in the afternoon. We walked across the street to the community center as parents arrived with pets.

Dogs barked, cats purred, and everyone was anxious to see one another's animals. There were parakeets, frogs, lizards, gerbils, and even fish. One dad even arrived with the family cow, Blossom, but they reminded him of the rules distributed at the start. Eventually Blossom was allowed to be tied up outside and was officially named the Precious Paws Pet Parade greeter.

The rest of the classes filed across the street and took a seat on the bleachers as members of the community showed up to enjoy the event too.

I was keeping a lookout for Mom and Aunt Ella to come with Patches and Moses. Anna and I had decorated special collars for them to wear. I knew they would both do a terrific job.

Signs were made to advertise the big fundraiser the next evening.

Help The Precious Paws Animal Shelter!

**Talent Show!
Auction!
Bake and Craft Sale!**

**Saturday, December 5th
6:00 p.m.**

I hugged my mom, dad, and Aunt Ella as they arrived with Patches and Moses. They both looked terrific and were glad to see all the people. Moses was especially happy to see me. Faith zipped this way and that, just as thrilled to see all the animals as everyone else. I laughed when she landed on the back of Moses to take her place in the parade.

"Woof! Woof!" Patches barked as Faith scratched him behind the ear.

Mr. O'Tool's marching band led the way when the parade began. The band played "Talk to the Animals" as the choir sang behind them, dressed in a variety of animal costumes.

The kids that brought stuffed animals had put together their own presentation to "Old McDonald Had a Farm," and it was a huge hit, thanks to the help of Mr. O'Tool.

It was so much fun. Several animals were rushed outside once in a while, causing big rounds of laughter from the crowd. Somebody's bird escaped, but no one seemed to mind as long as Jeremy Slavinski's snake remained safely in its cage.

The parade was a huge success! The animals

were well behaved. Other than Blossom, all the other animals were welcome and everyone had followed the rules regarding the type of animals that were invited. Mr. Duncan thanked everyone and finished the event by inviting them back for the fundraiser the following night.

There was just one problem: would there even be a fundraiser?

CHAPTER NINE

Raining Cats and Dogs

I got home with Moses right before the rain. I saw Mom, Dad, Anna, and Aunt Ella sitting in the kitchen, talking about the parade. Nicola shared with me all of the problems and things that still had to be done for the fundraiser after the parade. I was afraid to tell my mom and dad. They would say I was irresponsible again.

I sat on the front porch and watched the rain fall. Moses nuzzled up against me and whimpered.

"What is it, Moses?"

Faith flew around the corner and zoomed past me. She circled around and sat on Moses' back.

"Moses likes you a lot," she said.

"Yes," I answered." I like him a lot too."

"Remember why you named him Moses?"

"Sure," I said as Moses came over and laid his

head in my lap. He gazed at me with such a sweet look.

"Think, Katie, and have faith. Don't be afraid, Munchkin," she said.

"God helped Moses rescue the people from Egypt," I began as I reached out to pet the dog. I remembered how afraid I was that day on the ice when I reached out for the stick and Moses saved me.

"When God told Moses to save the people in Egypt, he was afraid," I told Faith, "just as I'm afraid to tell my mom and dad now."

"That's right," Faith said, "but God didn't let Moses down."

I smiled up at Faith. I loved her so much! "No, God helped Moses, just as He'll help me. I'm going to tell my mom and dad what's happening."

Faith flew over and gave me a little kiss. "You can do it, Munchkin."

It was time to be responsible and own up to what was happening, so I went into the house.

"Katie, the parade was marvelous!" Aunt Ella said.

"Yes, it was fun, wasn't it?" I asked, taking off Moses' leash so he could run freely around the house.

"Woof!"

"Ummm . . ." I began nervously. "I have something to tell you."

"Well have a seat, sweetheart," Daddy said.

They all looked at me expecting me to say something terrific, because that's all I had done for the last few weeks. Another glance at Faith gave me the courage to go on.

"Not everything is ready for tomorrow night," I began. "Even Nicola is disbusted!"

"Do you mean *disgusted*, honey?"

"Yes, that," I said. Then I told them about the things that still had to be done, about our meeting at lunch, and what Nicola told me after the parade. I told them how everyone was bickering and how upset Nicola was that the group hadn't been straight with her either. I even told them about my test and pet essay that had to be redone this weekend.

"I'm really sorry. We all tried so hard, but I guess you were right. We took on too much. I was irresponsible again."

I didn't want to look at them. I could feel their disappointment. There was a long awkward silence, and I refused to make eye contact.

"I'm seeing some responsibility," Daddy said.

"What?" I said, looking up at last.

"It took a lot of courage for you to tell us that.

By owning what you've done, you stepped up and took responsibility for it," he said.

"That's right," Mom agreed. "You worked very hard. The fact is we've been talking about that all week. We have to make a confession of our own."

"Huh?"

"As your parents, we should have taken more responsibility too. We should have insisted you keep things on a smaller scale or have gotten more involved ourselves. So we're sorry, too, honey."

This was not what I expected to hear!

"We're not condoning what you've done. You have to learn to budget your time better and understand how long you need to allow for homework and what you can get involved with. But we sure would like to help you with it."

Daddy came over to give me a hug, and we were joined by Mom, Anna, and Aunt Ella. As we did a group hug, I looked over to Faith who was smiling.

As we stood together, Aunt Ella led us in a short prayer. We asked that God bless our event and help us conquer the problems with courage and grace.

"Okay, we've got work to do!" Daddy said. "I suggest you start by calling Nicola. Why don't you ask her and the rest of your club members over. Tell Nicola to bring those notes."

"Your mother and I will get on the phone and recruit some parents to help fill in some of those missing pieces for tomorrow night," Aunt Ella said.

Things happened fast! I had trouble keeping up. Nicola and the others got to my house soon after my call. Nicola was thrilled to hear that help had arrived.

Several pizzas later the entire house was a whirlwind of activity. Programs were being typed, copied, and folded. The phone rang off the hook as parents responded to our call for help. At the end of the evening we were pooped but felt better about the event . . . until the phone rang one more time.

Aunt Ella hung up. The look on her face caused the entire room to grow silent.

"I have bad news," she said. "We may have to cancel after all."

CHAPTER TEN

Busy as a Bee

We all woke early the next day. It was a sunny, chilly day, much like the day I fell through the ice. I quickly dressed and went downstairs.

The call Aunt Ella received the night before was from the Shine Elementary School principal. A big truck had backed into an area that controlled all of the electricity for the school and community center. They didn't expect electricity to be restored until Monday.

Everybody thought it was a disaster, until my daddy came to the rescue. He called and got permission for us to use the Camp SonShine Center that he is in charge of on Lake Lightning. Everyone was super relieved. We already had so much to do that we still were not totally positive it would all get done on time.

"There's a lot to do, kiddo," Daddy said. "We have to fold programs, pick up the auction baskets

at the school, the crafts from Aunt Ella's, and ...
well, do whatever we can to get done before the
people start to arrive."

"Everything will turn out fine," Mom smiled.
Aunt Ella said she always looked on the bright side
of everything. "Do you know what you are going
to say when you and Moses go up on stage tonight,
sweetheart?"

"I think so."

"Hey, don't look so nervous. You're going to do

just fine, and if you do get stuck, you'll have Moses there to help you."

I rolled my eyes and made a face. She was not making me feel better.

"Just think of it as sharing your talent, like all the other kids who will be singing or juggling or whatever they have planned to do," Anna suggested.

"Not much of a talent," I said.

"What do you mean? It's a wonderful talent, Katie!" Daddy interrupted. "Listen, you've got a talent for caring about others, including animals. That's how this whole thing got started."

"I thought it all started when she fell through the ice?" Anna teased.

"Everything happens for a reason," Mom said. "Now both of you girls grab those bags and put them in the car. We've got to get going!"

• • •

We headed over to Aunt Ella's to collect the crafts. Then we went to the Camp SonShine Center. Lots of people showed up to help. The entire community was excited. I was so glad that I told Mom and Daddy what was really happening. Not only did things go smoother, but the Precious Girls Club no longer had to do all the work alone. Everyone pitched in.

By late afternoon, it was starting to get dark. Everybody was rushing this way and that, trying to get things done on time. Signs were up telling the audience how to get to the Camp SonShine area. Auction baskets were being wrapped and bowed. Bake sale items were getting tagged and displayed.

"Here's the last batch!" Aunt Ella said, bursting through the door with more crafts. "I just have to put a few finishing touches on a few of them, and they'll be ready to go."

"Oh my, Ella, these turned out lovely," Mom said.

"Thanks to all of the children and adults who turned up over the last few weeks to make them," Aunt Ella winked.

"Say, Ella, where did you put Moses before his big stage debut?" Daddy asked.

"Oh no! In my hurry to get these done and over here, I completely forgot to bring him with me. I'll have to go back and get him."

"What about the finishing touches?"

"I can get him," I offered. "I'm finished with all my stuff. I can run over to your house, put him on the leash, and we'll walk back to the camp."

"Oh, Katie, darlin', would you mind?" Aunt Ella asked.

"Of course not," I said, knowing that it would take my mind off being so nervous about going on stage. I hated just standing around waiting.

"Okay, sweetheart, but you'll have to hurry. You don't have that much time."

"I know, Mom. I'll be back in plenty of time."

She kissed me on the top of my head as I put on my hat and coat. "Thanks for your help. We appreciate it."

●　　●　　●

I rushed out into the chilly air without the slightest clue of what was ahead.

CHAPTER ELEVEN

Can You Teach an Old Dog New Tricks?

It was getting dark as Faith and I hurried toward the camp with Moses. He was such a happy, friendly dog. I could not help but wonder where he used to live.

"Woof! Woof, woof!" Moses barked as he suddenly pulled me in a different direction, tugging on his leash.

"No, Moses. We're not going that way. Come on boy, we have to get to the camp."

Moses would not listen. He continued to bark and pull me toward the glistening ice on Lake Lightning.

"Oh no! We're not going that way either. Come on now, Moses. If I'm late, I'm gonna get in super big trouble!"

"Woof! Woof!" Moses barked and tugged.

"Faith, what is he barking at?" I asked.

This was not like Moses. He usually listened really well and liked going for walks. I could not understand what was the matter with him—until I spotted the small dark figure on the ice. Had someone fallen in?

The minute I saw it, I let Moses pull me toward the lake as Faith followed behind. We raced for the shore. The cold air made my lungs hurt when I breathed. I strained to see as daylight melted into darkness, lit by the rising moon.

I was thankful it was not a person. But I was sad to see that a big black dog had fallen into the lake, just as I had several weeks ago. Because I'd learned so much about different animals at the Precious Paws Animal Shelter, I thought it looked like a black lab. The poor thing was doing her best to claw her way through the slippery ice and freezing water.

"Faith! She's caught in the ice, but I think it's keeping her from falling in and drowning."

Moses wanted to run out onto the ice, just like he had when he saved me. I pulled hard on his leash to keep him on the shore with me.

"What should I do, Faith? What do you think, Moses?"

"Woof, woof!"

"Why isn't anyone around when you need them?" I asked, feeling very frustrated.

"It's a little dark for most people to be out this way, Munchkin," Faith reminded me.

"I don't want to leave her to run all the way to the camp for help. But if I go out on the ice, I don't know if it will support me."

"When you don't know what to do, you can always say a little prayer, Katie," Faith said.

What was the responsible thing to do? One thing was for sure—making the right choice wasn't always easy. So I listened to Faith and I prayed.

CHAPTER TWELVE

In the Dog House

"Where is she?" Katie's mom asked, as she tried to smile and greet people arriving for the big night. "What time is it?"

"Don't get your britches in a bunch," Aunt Ella joked, trying to lighten the mood. "She'll be here. She probably lost track of the time rough-housing with Moses. She loves playing with that dog. Besides, I see that Mr. Duncan is late too."

"You know how nervous she was about going on stage tonight, honey. Moses will help take her mind off things," Katie's dad reassured her.

"The two of you don't fool me," Katie's mom answered. "I can see the worried looks on your faces too."

"What time *is* it?" Aunt Ella whispered to Katie's dad.

"Twenty minutes after six o'clock," he said, frustrated and worried himself.

None of them could stop looking toward the door.

"Anna, please call your sister again," Mom asked. "Try Aunt Ella's and our house, too, just in case she went there for something."

"Okay, Mom."

While Anna made the calls, the crowd mingled about the room placing bids on the beautiful baskets and purchasing the wonderfully handmade crafts.

"There was no answer," Anna told her parents and aunt. "But don't worry. Even though Katie is nervous about getting up in front of everybody, tonight is really important to her and her friends. She wouldn't miss it for anything."

"Thanks, sweetheart," Anna's mom said, giving her a little hug.

"Is Katie okay, Mrs. Bennett?" Nicola asked.

She and the girls had gathered near the stage, getting ready as the crowd began taking their seats for the show.

"I'm sure she's fine, just running a little late," Mr. Bennett answered, "just like Mr. Duncan."

"Well, we're almost ready to start. The reporter for the *Shine Times* was asking about them."

"Tell him he'll know they are here the minute we do," Aunt Ella said, ushering Nicola back over to her friends. She knew the questions were only making it worse for Katie's parents.

"I think you should go look for her," Mom said quietly, as the school band began warming up.

"Then Daddy will miss everything if she comes while he's gone, Mom!" Anna protested.

"She should have been here fifteen or twenty minutes ago. How long do you think we should wait?" Mom asked.

The lights flickered, causing the rest of the crowd to find a seat. There was still no sign of Katie.

"We'll have to start without her, Mrs. Bennett," Nicola said, sounding disappointed. "I'm really sorry. I'm sure she can start the second half of the show right after intermission though."

"Thank you, Nicola. I'm sure that will work out just fine," Katie's mom answered.

As the first act was introduced, Aunt Ella looked at Mr. and Mrs. Bennett. What could have happened to Katie?

CHAPTER THIRTEEN

Look What the Cat Dragged In

The sound of applause filled the Camp SonShine Center as the third act in the talent show completed their number.

"What are we going to do?" asked Katie's mom.

Reaching for his coat, Katie's dad said, "I'll find her, honey, don't worry. Ella, would you please stay

with Marlene and Anna? I'll call the minute I find Katie."

"Umm . . . Dad," said Anna.

"Not now, sweetheart! It will have to wait."

"But look!"

As I walked through the door, my mom jumped up from her chair and practically ran me over.

"Mom! You're suffocating me," I mumbled, buried deep within her bulky winter sweater. She squeezed me so tight I was fighting for air.

"Where have you been?" she demanded, pulling herself away from me.

Mom, Dad, Aunt Ella, and Anna all waited for me to respond. Each of the girls from my club quietly wandered over to see what had happened. At the same time, the crowd erupted with applause as another act finished on stage. But instead of the master of ceremonies introducing the next act, everyone had turned their attention on me!

The next thing I knew it was my turn on stage,

only the story I was telling wasn't the one about falling through the ice a few weeks ago.

"Hi, everybody," I started as some of my friends peeked out from the curtain backstage. "Thank you all for coming to the fundraiser for the Precious Paws Animal Shelter. The Precious Girls Club really appreciates all the help we got from everyone.

"I know I was supposed to tell you about how a dog named Moses rescued me from falling through the ice on Lake Lightning a few weeks ago. Hopefully you already read about it in the paper.

"Tonight I was on my way here with Moses when we saw a dog trapped out on the very same ice I fell through. I didn't really know what to do. I figured if I ran all the way here to tell my mom and dad, that it would be too late. But I've also been learning a lot about responsibility lately."

I took a deep breath and looked at Faith who was flitting back and forth over the bake sale table in the back of the room. She liked sweets a lot! She gave me a smile, a wink, and made me smile too.

CHAPTER FOURTEEN

A Dog Gone Success!

I looked out at the crowd and saw all the people who cared about me. I really didn't feel all that nervous anymore. So I took another big breath and got ready to finish my story.

"I knew it wasn't very responsible to go back out on the ice, even though a dog was in trouble. But I also felt that I wouldn't be responsible leaving her to get my mom or dad. Then I remembered that the animal shelter is just over the hill next to the lake. So I ran to see if Mr. Duncan could help."

As I told that part of the story, Mr. Duncan came out from backstage with Moses and a big black lab, both on leashes. Everybody clapped and the newspaper photographer started taking lots of pictures.

"I think I learned that being responsible means not only following the rules, but also doing what we can to help others. That's what tonight is all about—doing our best to help animals. So that's what I did when I saw the dog in the lake. I did the best I could, and Mr. Duncan and a friend of his from the rescue team knew just what to do. I hope you will do your best to help take care of the animals in Shine, Wisconsin. If you don't have an animal to take care of, there are lots of animals that need your help at the Precious Paws Animal Shelter. Thank you!"

People clapped really loud and even stood up. It made Moses and the pretty black dog both bark and everybody laughed. I'm pretty sure that my mom, dad, Aunt Ella, and Faith were clapping the loudest.

After the show Mr. Duncan thanked all of us for our help. He couldn't believe the huge success of our event.

After everyone was gone, Aunt Ella gave each of us a little gold star to add to our bracelets. She told us she was very proud of us and the responsibility we had shown. Then we presented Nicola with a little gift. She did such a great job organizing the event. She opened up the box and took out a beautiful, sparkling snow globe with an angel inside. Winding it up, the music played and the angel danced around the snowy white.

"Her name is Victoria," I said. "Without you, our event would never have been victorious."

Nicola didn't know what to say. She loved the pretty angel and thanked us over and over again.

•   •   •

We were exhausted when we got home. It was quite a night but a huge success. We raised a ton of money for the Precious Paws Pet Shelter.

"I have a surprise for the two of you," Daddy

said to Anna and me. He opened a box and removed a little kitten. "This is Sparky," he said. "Your mom and I agreed that the two of you have shown enough responsibility to care for him."

It was a gorgeous black-and-white kitten! We were full of thank-yous as we took turns holding our new family member. Everyone was thrilled— well, except for Patches. I think he was a little jealous, but he would learn to love Sparky too.

After we settled down to say goodnight to one another, my mom finished by saying this poem:

We've had a busy, hectic day
But now it's time for us to pray.
And as we tuck you into bed,
We bend to kiss your little head.
You're full of love, your future is bright.
We ask God's love for you tonight.
We want to take away your fear,
And always hold you, oh, so near!
You make us proud, it's very true.
Our precious daughters, we love you!

Up next for the
Precious Girls Club: Book # 4

The Best Gift of All

Avery excused herself from her party and went to the restroom. Once there, she washed her hands, stood in front of the mirror, and touched her newly pierced ears. She fanned out her fingers to look at the sparkly polish on them.

Twirling around, she caused her pretty pink dress to swirl about in the air. All of a sudden another door opened.

Avery jumped! She had no idea she was not alone.

Read more in The Best Gift of All
in stores Summer 2009

A Charmed
Life Is Precious

Make a beautiful bracelet that tells your story and shows how precious you truly are.

Responsible Charm

We earned our Responsible charm in Project Precious Paws! Being Responsible makes you a star!

Loving Charm

Helpful Charm

Kind Charm